# Bully's Foe

**" Undefeated Bully who Changed Miraculously "**

- James E. Benedict

# Acknowledgement

I want to thank my dear friend Abhinav Gupta for the tremendous illustrations.

"We have only just begun," as the song goes.

Thanks to my lovely wife and amazing children to whom I have told stories to, for many years. I'm thrilled God has helped my son Noah, a medical miracle. Also, thanks to Lori, the brilliant science professor who carried me through proofreading. Thanks to Mousumi Dey for the management. Lastly, I thank God who gives the inspiration to write.


- James E. Benedict

# Author

# James E. Benedict

Is a teacher, writer and storyteller. He is the founder of Emmanuel Literacy Foundation. James is also the author of Unlikely Friends, The Contest, The Mystery Box and is working on many more books. His stories shows goodness can come in hopeless situations. James travels, teaches and inspires people in several countries and cultures.

# Bully's Foe

Seventeen-year-old Rod Becker focused down the hallway calculating when the principal, the guidance counselor, secretary or music teacher would come out first. Whoever appeared would allow him to plan for his next assault. From his cube head, Rod's neck was so thick, it made his form look bullet-shaped. Muscles were stacked on top of one another. Rod's face was sprinkled with acne that ended with a red lump on his shovelnose. He had his followers but he was not Hollywood material. Students, faculty and the police considered: 'Were there any known weaknesses?' One came as a surprise.

While clumps of students moved between classes Rod approached a row of lockers. He pried, Faith Holiday, one of his ex-girlfriends, "Can't you see me anymore?"

The tall, bright student girl countered, "Don't you know the judge said you can't talk to me?"

A girl in white skirt used scissors to split a chocolate bar as her classmate peeked over her shoulder. With an audience looking on from neighboring lockers, Rod muttered, "We all make mistakes!"

He strutted away with continual thoughts of revenge, scribbling a note on his tablet. After harassing Faith, Rod remained relentless in taunting others, sticking his index finger in an All State soccer player's chest, "The only reason you're a star is because I play football."

 After the confrontation with the soccer star, Faith nudged between two students, "We always come and go in fear of you. Becker, you trap us until you find someone else to harass..."

She rubbed a flow of tears on her sports shirt. Rod couldn't let her get away without having the last word, "You're not innocent honey."

He strutted away seemingly untouched by any pain.

Before the day was complete three guys surrounded him in Biology class. One blurted out, "Looks just like him without the mustache, a Fu Manchu, the devil's horns and antlers."

Rod sketched the principal. He excelled in art, but often missed the first period, because he was hurling massive barbells in his backyard. The athlete regularly wheeled to school on his unicycle. Rod scored mysteriously high on tests, driving both students and teachers to near insanity.

The frail junior Mark Weinstein, like Rodney, could be seen everywhere in the school. In the gym he created statistics out of sports. Round shouldered, with thick glasses, Mark led the chess club to the National Finals. Cornell and Stanford wanted him. He was offered a sizable grant to Yale University. The young student some called "The Book" was considering becoming a cancer research scientist.

During the last period study hall, Rod went to the library for a study guide of Gulliver's Travels. Mark came into the library minutes before and was checking out the last copy. Strangely intimidating for Rod was Mark. He was paper-thin, looked perpetually tired with a long nose and thin hazel hair interwoven with gray streaks. Rodney could never strike Mark. Wind could blow him over.

"Oh I really need that Monarch Note, Mark."

Mark threw his backpack on the counter, rubbed his chin and cheek, then stuffed the study guide into his overloaded backpack, "Sorry I was here first. Try Barnes and Noble."

Who would dare to deny Rod? The budding scholar Mark Weinstein, being logical, straightforward and pure in heart was a rare case.

"Can we have a cup of coffee together in the cafeteria Mark? I had some questions about biology. I really need your help."

Mark glimpsed at Rod. His lips moved then he pushed the words out in monotone while a slight smile appeared, "All right."

They strolled to the cafeteria. Rod led the way towards the windows that faced the lake. It was several tables away from the coffee table.

Rod shook his wrist, "My arm got hurt in a ball game. Can you grab the coffee?"

"Sure," lonely Mark said, with great optimism.

Rod took three crumpled bills out of his wallet and threw them towards Mark.

"Here I'll buy."

"Thanks, Rod."

Mark laid down his backpack and scooped up the money.

"Do you like sugar?"

"Can't live without it, Ten spoons aren't enough." Rod said.

Mark thought, 'That's why he's so aggressive.'

When Mark began pouring coffee in both cups, his back faced Rod.

Rod meticulously zipped open Mark's backpack. He slipped the study guide out, slid it between the pages of his English book, then secured Mark's backpack. His eyes never left the budding scholar.

Mark squeezed the lids shut and faithfully brought the coffee to Rod.

Rod stood slightly off the chair, "Oh Mark, I forgot my appointment at Mr. Hall's room." Rodney Becker darted out of the cafeteria. Mark got home to discover the book had disappeared.

Four days later a terror strike came on an otherwise cloudless summer day. The school was readying for a speech on Argentina by Mr. Hall after lunch. Rod burst into the cafeteria. The muscle man calculatingly chewed gum and glimpsed around. "No security or teachers", he observed. He wore a tight white Adidas shirt, baggy Levis and a chain that dangled from his rope belt to his long back pocket wallet. Most of the students were eating rubbery pizza, which was pita bread, a plop of tomato sauce with a sprinkle of cheese. It was harder to swallow than gummy bears.

Tim McCall, a senior and star basketball player, sat with his brother Ed, a sophomore. Both boys wore long faces.

Canadian geese flew by in peaceful patterns landing in the school's pond. Rod shoved aside several students in the food line. The McCalls were studious athletes that never officially dated, but Dominica Verdi walked home with Tim once. She coaxed him into going out for ice cream. Dominica had bright cheeks, shoulder length hair and was a basketball cheerleader. Tim didn't know Rod had gone to McDonald's with her the week before. Rod heard about the Tim and Dominica outing from another football player. The school bully strutted over to the table with an artificial smile. The ballplayers from the surrounding two tables paused eating, talking or looking at text books.

"Hi guys." Instantly Rod's face transformed into a murderous look, one you might see on a serial killer.

"Hi Rod," scattered voices said respectfully. Something was wrong. Fear gripped the crowd.

Tim, the star center, searched inside for reasons why Rod would trouble him. Rod probed deep into McCall's eyes like a prize fighter looking to strike.

Rod's voice trumpeted. "I hear you saw Dominica?"

Tim looked slightly up while sitting as Rod stood over him. When standing side-by-side Rod looked up at the young man as you would a street light overhead. Rod was five foot eleven, two hundred and thirty five pounds. The giant Tim and his brother at the next table were the tallest and perhaps thinnest basketball players from miles around towering at six foot four and six-five. Over a hundred students were scattered in the cafeteria. From Rod's expression a ripple effect happened, it got progressively quiet. No teachers were present yet.

Tim knew the threatening look. Rod's reputation was…growing even further. He was jealous, vindictive and violently predictable. Rod strutted around the way royalty would. Tim considered how to reason with the muscleman.

He mumbled with lengthy pauses between each sentence,

"Never meant any harm. We just had ice cream. Sorry."

He reached out his right hand begging desperately for a handshake. The fuming muscleman kept his hands on his sides. Rod studied Tim's cheek line, his nose and his mouth. Tim began coughing and covered his mouth.

The basketball player desperately wanted Rod to understand.

With control, Rod said slowly, while tapping his chest, "She's mine."

Tim's eyes stared down hopelessly in his coffee. Struggling to get the soft words out, Tim finally said, "Sorry, I didn't know."

14

With a tiger's rage, Rod yanked the peaceful athlete's hair forward, slamming his head into the giant Seven-Eleven Styrofoam cup of hot coffee. The cup exploded under the weight. A loud thump from Tim's head hitting the table echoed around the neighboring tables.

"No." Tim cried out, his face soaked with coffee.

"Leave him alone," said one sullen voice.

Another pleaded, "Stop it." Students were forced to stand up in protest. Several voices chanted injustice.

Rod wasn't satisfied. He considered nothing Tim could say would right "going out with his property."

While Tim was slowly raising his head, Rod climbed with his knees on the table, dragging the center's head forward. Then he swung Tim's body across the table with more anger and power than an enraged tiger. A usually timid longhaired basketball guard attempted to shove Rod out of the way. The muscleman bulldozed him with one arm. Then he threw four punches in succession hitting Tim in the stomach once, chest twice and the last connected with his jaw. The last punch ricocheted off Tim's jaw to his mouth onto the guard attempting to help.

One bald Spanish cook, with the body of a bowling ball, was preparing food. He heard screams and rolled to the scene. A small blond choir teacher was singing with two students at the back of the cafeteria. He raced over, shoving students against the lunch line rail.

"Excuse me. Move aside. Move over."

Several plates of food toppled. Tomato sauce, pudding, vegetables, pizza, spoons and forks flipped off the trays. A collage of color coated the floor. After racing through the crowd the men tugged Rod away from the injured center. Tim struggled to pick up his body. A shower of blood from his nose coated his shirt. The injured guard scurried beneath the table. Confused, embarrassed and lying on the floor he refused to get up.

"What happened here, Mr. Becker?" a muscular gym teacher asked searching Rod's eyes for an excuse.

15

"You better…" Rod fought to catch his breath. "You better ask him."

The teacher yelled, pointing in Rod's chest. "I'm not asking him, I'm asking you."

Rod chewed gum as quick as a machine gun, and then opened up, "He should have known not to date someone else's girlfriend."

"You are not king of this school. You don't own every girl. Come down to the principal's office with me. You've got problems."

Mumbling began to spread throughout the cafeteria.

A chain smoking Science teacher approached Tim, "Let's go to the nurse. He'll get his."

Rod Becker never seemed to, "Get his." He would get in trouble and sift back into school as innocent as a nun. Male students were terrorized and teachers became baffled, seeking a solution to handle Rod's behaviour. He damaged some physically. Others were crushed with raw intimidation. It had been incidents recorded in Principal Durbin's log that dragged the school's reputation lower than a jail. Rod cursed faithful principal Durbin's sleep.

The principal informed Rod's mother on the phone, "Your son has been suspended again Mrs. Becker."

"Suspended again?" Rod's mom said, fingering a dental pick on her part time job as a dental assistant. "Did he get caught popping bubbles in the hall?"

"No. He punched an honor student several times and another student too. It's been his third and fourth assault charges."

"You're lucky you have my son. He wins all the art contests and he's an All American Football player. Rod's put your school in the papers more than one time."

"Lucky?" Durbin wiped his brow. He continued, about to weep, "There are many good private schools that could use Rod's talents."

Durbin cleared his throat then pleaded. "We know you can afford the best, your son has great potential."

The principal began to tear open some aluminum packets and chewed some chalky white stomach medicine.

"He likes the school. We talked about sending him to St. Peter's. Rod refuses to leave public school. My husband and I will talk about this, but he's on another business trip. We rarely see him."

17

"He'll have to stay home for a few days, Mrs. Becker. Do you want to come in and discuss it with the Vice Principal and me?"

After finishing with the dental pick, Rod's mom strolled to the Dentist's small cafeteria area eyeing some cheesecake. "I'm sorry my boy's a little rough. We're trying. There's no need for me to see you."

"Thanks." principal Durbin answered, feeling a temporary victory in the everlasting School versus Becker battle. He gave a thumb's up sign to his secretary.

"My son's a good boy!" Becker's mom combated the principal with the same story, like a key stuck on the computer. "The school just doesn't know how to deal with him."

Mr. Durbin, with short silver hair and drooping bags under his eyes, hung up the phone. He lay back in his office chair, hoping for this latest episode to be over. Durbin considered early retirement. His calendar was marked counting the days when Rod would graduate.

He snapped his finger at his secretary, rubbed his forehead and pointed to the door for Rod to come in.

The principal's secretary summoned the muscleman, "Rod, the principal's ready to see you."

Rod's Adidas shirt had a smudge of blood by his ribs. Rod held a skateboard as he entered. He looked at Mr. Durbin slouched in his red leather office chair, his head cocked back like he was suffering whiplash. The athlete searched the room then sat on a metal gray chair next to two file cabinets.

The principal struggled out the words, "We meet again Mr. Becker."

"What's the verdict, pop?" Rod began.

The principal moved his head up, looked at Rod, shaking his head. He began, "You have been in trouble for two years straight. Your parents have to deal with this daily. We have to put you out of school for five days."

A mustached retired detective, now head of school security, was standing outside the door. He shuffled in without knocking.

"Quiet," said Harding, the tall detective with eyes that constantly roved wherever he went.

"He's the principal. Call him sir, not pop."

Rod didn't reply. He chewed gum while crossing his arms. The detective continued, "It seems you struck two students Mr. Becker?"

Rod's eyes bounced off the secretary to the detective and onto the principal.

"I'll try not to do it again."

The officer stood before Rod, and then began, "You have a rap sheet with assault of seven students, biting, gouging one student's eye during a football game, threatening female students and about twelve legal charges that never stuck."

 Rod continued to chew his gum with a repulsive look. He clenched his fist like he was about to strike the detective.

"Son," With folded arms leaning against Durbin's rusty gray file cabinet, the detective began again, "You're on a bad road. You'll end up in jail Rod."

Rod's eyes flickered up at the officer then down on a box of plaques used to award fine students. Rod liked them and was elated when he got a few, but knew this was not the occasion.

"Spit the gum out", the officer ordered Rod.

Rod roared back, "Is it against the law to chew? Tell your son to spit it out,

I have my own father." Rod answered, continuing to clinch his right fist tightly.

The detective wanted to get up and react. Then he remembered, "Never hit or fight with a student unless being threatened."

The seasoned detective screamed and turned red, "You're being stupid."

His mouth opened wide and as animated as a cartoon, with a final barrage of comments, "I see teens like you go to jail. That's what'll happen to you. You have to change. Do you understand, Rod?"

Rod clasped his hands together on his lap. Exhausted from the many confrontations with Rod Becker the principal ended the meeting, "Find out what pages you'll be covering in class, then please study at home."

"OK Principal."

"If you get into any trouble during the next five days, you will be permanently dismissed from school."

The principal was distraught then shared with Rod, "Tim's parents are going to file some legal charges against you. He had to go to the emergency room. I tried to calm things down, Rod"

Rod stood up, "That means I can't come back?"

"If any more problems happen, you'll never step on school property again."

Fiery Rod quickly opened up another stick of gum and began chewing it.

The following morning the principal arrived at school while teachers and office people trickled in. Middleborough High had a sprawling lawn with a murky lake across from the front doors. Frogs, fish and ducks made it feel like nature was the school's closest neighbor.

A towering, longhaired blond female guidance counselor thumped loudly on Durbin's door.

"What is it?" the principal answered, raising his voice.

She opened the door and stuck her head in. "Someone took the American Flag down and put a pirate flag up." She bit her lip attempting to hold in her laughter.

"It's not funny." He rebuked the young woman.

"Sorry." She said shutting her mouth. The young lady considered losing her first job out of college.

Principal Durbin jumped off his chair, dashed out of his office, then out the nearest door. Just a few feet out the door he looked up and saw the painful joke.

"That idiot," he howled.

There was no sign of the American Flag that proudly flew over the school. The sixty-seven year old head custodian, nicknamed Red, hoisted it every day at six. In its place was this mammoth, skull and crossbones on a flowery bed sheet.

The principal inquired, "Where's faithful Red now? Perhaps he knows something about this?"

His name, Red, stuck from during his youth. His red hair was as orange as a sunset, now it turned a dusty gray.

The secretary answered, "It's not likely, he's almost deaf. Red comes in, starts in the cafeteria and doesn't leave there for almost an hour. Then he takes a break in the custodian's office before he punches in."

"A dog froze to death near the front door last winter and Red never noticed."

School security questioned people that started their business early. A local roofer was guzzling coffee in his office.

"Did you see anyone on the high school grounds before you got to work?"

"Yes, I did." A bright smile filled his pudgy face. "There was some nut, dressed like a Ninja Warrior, with a black sheet shimming up the flagpole. I was driving to the office.

"What time was it?"

"About six thirty. Someone must have dared him."

"Was anyone with him?"

"Not that I saw." The contractor answered, looking at the wall clock.

"I have to get on the road. Sorry."

"Just one more question, did he have a bicycle? Did you see a car outside?"

"I just got a glimpse, sorry."

"Rod doesn't…" The principal hastily interrupted then paused, "Go ahead."

The maintenance staff was forced to cut the flagpole rope, which had over twenty knots at the bottom.

The next day was peaceful until lunchtime.

Suddenly the fire alarm wailed loudly causing everyone to hold their ears.

A fire truck raced, with lights flashing and sirens screaming, to Middleborough High.

"Mr. Durbin", the school nurse said, grabbing the older man's arm dashing into the cafeteria, "There's a big problem."

"What problem?" Durbin said, while he chewed on a chicken bone and listened to soft flute music on his ear buds.

"Your office caught fire!"

He stood up spreading his arms out with bulging eyes, "Caught fire."

"Yes. Students saw someone dressed in an Indian costume sitting on one of the islands in the lake shooting flaming arrows into your office."

"You're crazy."

"No. I'm not."

"Who saw it?"

A frightened ninth grade boy joined them, shadowed by the nurse.

"I was near the lake eating a sandwich. The person was wearing this Indian outfit and had black and red make-up covering his face."

Durbin struggled back to the office, where smoke filled the hall. Teachers were coughing.

A loud voice sprung out, "Everyone leave the building."

Students exited the rooms and were beginning to assemble outside in the parking lot. Some were next to the lake. Two firemen in their helmets and orange raincoats stayed in the principal's office. A few more assembled outside, folding the hose back.

The books on his shelf looked like large slices of burnt toast. Putrid black water dripped from the shelves, a coffee pot and a microwave oven were melted. An overwhelming smell of burnt plastic and toasted books filled Durbin's office.

He reached up to his head, putting both hands on top. "My wife told me to retire a few years ago. I've done everything I could."

He reached down and began cracking his knuckles. Then he held up his index finger. The principal began to break up, crying out while addressing the younger school nurse.

"Rodney Becker. Rodney Becker. Just one student."

He opened up his hands, looked above and in a whimper begged, "Help me."

His face turned bright red then he held his chest.

The soft spoken nurse pitied the principal as if he were her father, thinking, "He should be spending his later years peacefully, strolling around a golf course with other retirees."

She ushered him out of his smoky burnt office to the grass outside and laid him down. His head rested against a tree. The vice principal and several of the teachers paced to the lake looking out at the small island full of reeds. Two skinny trees arose, one on top of the other. The grass sloped down into the murky water. A frog was croaking. Several teachers were on muddy ground searching the island. A History teacher in blue corduroys and a gray and red rugby shirt bent down and picked up a rock and hurled it into the water next to the island.

"Send someone around to the other side," The vice principal hollered.

Two math teachers, a guidance counselor and the computer teacher ran on a dirt path that leads to the other side.

At one thirty the principal's wife carried her husband's tormented soul away from his school. Durbin, hiding tears, staggered with his head drooping. A sickly whimper eeked out. "Can you call the police to Becker's house now?" he asked the retired detective.

The ordinarily friendly vice principal took his place.

The principal added, "His family lives on Spruce, about seven blocks away. Get cars to go behind the house, too, sirens off."

"Does he drive?" the treasurer asked.

"Not legally." The vice principal paused, spitting in the lake. Several Canadian geese flew over honking.

"Excuse me. He takes his father's car out."

At just past two, four police cars nosed in on Rod's house. Two stayed on Pine Street to peer into his back yard while two pulled in front of the one-family brick house.

A few officers marched up the slate path to the front door. They rang the bell. No answer. An overweight officer rubbed his chin, and then banged on the door. Still there was no response. Both officers walked around the house peeking in the windows and over the stockade fence. The in-ground swimming pool's motor hummed quietly. A small grey utility shed stood against the back fence. Two officers watched the house from the backside.

"Hope we got here in time. I mean did the kid have the time to get home?"

"Thirty minutes is plenty of time. He's practically a world-class sprinter. Rod's probably inside drinking a milkshake."

Detective Harding checked a few businesses en route to Rod's home. He questioned a bent backed woman with frizzy grey hair at Brady's Lumber,

"Did you see anything strange recently?"

She answered, squinting through her bifocals,

"Yes. She stumbled slowly through the words, "I saw a man about six feet, running through the neighborhood with an Indian outfit on."

"You know the star football player Becker?"

"Yes. He stopped in a few times with his dad." She sneezed, reached in a pale brown pocketbook and blew her nose. "Everybody knows the football star." she replied.

Two tractor-trailers, louder than locomotives filled with fresh lumber backed into the lumberyard. Their backup systems beeped obnoxiously. The screen door to the office was left open.

"Could it have been him?" the detective inquired.

The clerk yelled, "Sorry, I couldn't hear you."

Harding yelled, "Could it have been Rod Becker?"

With the trucks creeping to the back, the clerk also continued in a loud tone,

"I guess it could have. He looked strong and ran like the devil."

"Thanks." The detective jumped in his car.

The fire chief's station wagon pulled up to Becker's family home.
Detective Harding parked across the street. Wearing jeans and a plaid
shirt, scratching his shoulder, the chief left the door to the police station
wagon open. He approached the policemen, "Is the boy around?"

"No sign of him."

Both police and firemen were leaving when Mrs. Becker turned the
corner and rolled into the driveway in her olive BMW Coupe.

"What's wrong?" She whispered wearing dark sunglasses, a bright
yellow skirt and a satin blouse.

Detective Harding said, "There has been some trouble at school and we need to talk to Rod. He was suspended. The rule is he should be at home."

Lulu answered, "I'll go inside and see if he's around."

Harding, the fire chief and the two officers on-duty paced Becker's front lawn. Lulu Becker opened the front door and went inside.

"Rod, are you here?" Mom called out but still nothing.

She took a few minutes, then reappeared in the doorway,

"I'll search the house. He likes to play these games."

"What did he do?"

"Was he painting anything here recently?"

Rod's mom answered with a bright smile, "No. But I never know what Rod is doing in the basement, attic or garage. He's always making something."

The detective answered, pointing down the long street towards the lake, in the direction of the school. "Someone stole the American flag and put a pirate flag in its place. Now someone shot something flammable into the principal's office." He paused. "The principal's office caught fire."

"Does he play with a bow and arrow?" one officer continued.

Lulu struggled with words, "He, oh Rod, he dabbles in a lot of sports."

She continued, "You don't think my Rodney would do that?"

"You know your son. The person was dressed in an Indian outfit. The size and build matched your son", the detective answered.

She looked disappointed, and then replied angrily, "My son's a great student and a star athlete." Then she shouted, "Why do you keep accusing him of some new crime?"

The detective reached his both hands out, "Your son has the record to prove it. Students were in school. Besides the principal and Rod just had another run in."

Rod's mother opened the door to his room. Four glass tanks with piranhas, spiders, mice and one garden snake were neatly aligned on a massive metal desk. Plastic bats appeared to be flying, suspended by clear fishing lines. Rod's ceiling was highlighted with illuminated stars shining on black wallpaper. Two blown up photos, one of a former President and one with Rod putting his arm around the principal after winning a football game were pasted on the wall. Several darts were in both of Rod's photos. A few were even in Rod. The posters were decayed from being hit so many times. A block of surfboard wax covered Rod's picture with the principal. She searched, but no Rod.

"Rodney."

A muffled voice drifted through the bathroom door, "I'm taking a bath."

Mom opened the door slightly. A gush of steam flowed out.

"How come you didn't answer?"

"The water's running."

Mrs. Becker motored through the house to face the men outside.

"Sorry, he's taking a bath. Do you want to talk to him?"

"Yes ma'am. That's why we came," the detective said slowly stroking his mustache. She scurried back to the bathroom.

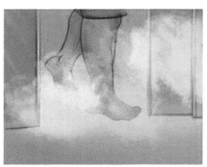

"Rodney, please come out." Lulu Becker stood outside the bathroom door, shaking her head. She whispered, "Rod, you're really creative. Why do you curse your father and me?"

Lulu took out her cell phone and keyed in her husband.

"It'll be alright mom."

"Well hurry." Lulu stroked her hair gently. "You're giving the principal nightmares. You got more enemies. One day you're not gonna get out of something."

"We'll work it out", Rod said.

Rod tramped out of the bathroom with striped lavender sweatpants and a matching sweatshirt.

"Dad's not answering his phone. I'll contact him later. Let's talk to the men outside."

Lulu held Rod's hand tightly as they exited the door. The screen door snapped shut behind them. All eyes probed Rod.

The fire chief dug in with folded arms, "Where have you been during lunchtime Rodney?"

"Been here. The school told me to stay home. I had to oblige." His eyes dropped away from the chief to the lawn. It grew quiet for a small eternity.

"Just finished my English homework and was going to start on my math, but I got tired, so I took a bath."

The detective began, "Someone has been causing trouble at school this morning, and now a fire in the principal's office. The flagpole incident wasn't serious, Rodney, the fire was."

"What fire? Fires are dangerous," Rod interrupted.

The detective continued. His words came out quickly and louder, "Rod, we've had enough. No one else has any reason to trouble the principal. You don't like him. He's not a bad man, maybe like your grandfather. We found something. They'll check fingerprints."

Rod shuffled his feet on the front porch, glimpsing away from the detective to the houses across the street.

A green Volvo wagon crept up to the stop sign at the corner. Then a light blue van appeared on the opposite side. Two women got out of the van. One woman went to the back seat and cradled a sleeping infant. A minivan bus with its engine revving swung around the corner, its yellow lights turned red. Children exited the bus.

Lulu opened up, "Can I speak to you men for a moment, alone?"

She ushered the detective and chief to the side yard. "Rod you stay on the porch," she commanded, pointing a foot away from her son's chest.

Rod shot back, "Don't be against me."

She glimpsed back with a torn look, "I'm your mother," she answered.

Her eyes flickered between the chief and the detective then began. "I'll pay for any damages."

"Arson's a felony" the chief said shaking his head slightly.

He continued, "I'm an electrician by trade. I was rewiring a house. The building inspector will be there tomorrow. That job can't be late, Mrs. Becker."

He looked at her and nudged the man next to him, "Mr. Fisher Is a city police officer and needs to be at work. The other men have jobs and families too."

The detective extended his open hand before Lulu, "If the prints are his he will have to suffer whatever the court says."

Lulu insisted. "I'll talk to him."

She left the men and went inside with Rod.

"Rod, when they find your prints, you're cooked." She slapped Rodney on the cheek.

"No way, I wore..." Rod looked deep in Lulu's eyes.

His mother knew Rod's mind. Lulu screeched, with a downcast expression, "You wore gloves, Rodney."

The men outside heard Lulu as clear as the president addressing the nation on television. Because Rod's father's company donates a lot of money to the alumni, there always seems to be one more dose of grace available to Rod.

"Can we get my son to sign something? We don't want trouble." Tears broke out from Lulu.

She dropped her pocket book, opened up her arms, palms opened, while she turned to Rod, "Please help me this time. Dad isn't going to let this one go easily."

The young man, undefeated in most of his epochs, had nailed his coffin shut this time.

Looking at the ground, he turned away from everyone, hugging the cold fence on the side yard.

Harding walked over to Rod, placing his hand on his shoulder and began whispering, "Do you know how many enemies you have in the school, in the police department, in the fire department, in other schools?" The chief moved a foot away from Harding.

"A lot," he said.

The fire chief called the men, "OK men. It's time we talk about what to do with Mr. Becker."

The detective called out, "Please stay here with your son, Mrs. Becker."

"We'll be here."

Lulu began weeping like a bereaved wife. Lulu reached into her pocketbook, took out a cigarette and put it between her index and middle finger ready to light it. She threw it unlit on the lawn.

The men assembled in an oval shape on the road. Rod and Lulu stayed on the slate path, just before the front steps.

Lulu raised her voice, "Rod, if they put you away, it's your fault." Rod, not wanting to look defeated, knew he deserved punishment.

He mumbled back, "They have no proof I wasn't studying."

A sporty blue Nissan, with music blasting, rounded the corner. Five high school boys peered out at Rod's house. They turned the music down while jockeying their way through the police and fire chief's cars. The car crawled to the end of the street as the boys stared back at the scene.

The chief began whispering to the men before him.

"We have to punish Rodney. No light rebuke will alter his behavior."

"What about his dad?" the vice principal said, staring at the sewer ditch on the road.

"Are we going to live under Becker blackmail forever?" the detective asked.

Several, "No's" echoed through the company of men.

"Rod won't do time for arson." The chief continued, while slowly shaking his head, "He has to get caught in the act."

The detective started to turn red. He sweated. His voice became raspy as he punched his opened hand, "We couldn't get him to sign when he put a hose into Sheriff Murdock's car and flooded the whole thing. The stinking car became a fishbowl." They began ushering Rod into the detective's car. He remained calm during questioning.

Lulu shouted with an erratic, violent look, "Don't touch my son!"

Rod stayed in the car for twenty minutes, then the men opened the back door and Rod went quietly inside his home. Both Harding and the chief's eyes followed the young man slowly inside his house. All remained silent. Lulu waved to the men.

Harding said, "We'll search the house, get a DNA check on the bow, search for the Indian outfit."

The vice-principal, bent over and began mumbling, "Police never get Becker."

For one last huddle, the detective, the chief, plain duty police officers and a few other men from the school remained on the road, discussing the day's events. They left in different directions, on different missions, none wearing a smile.

All the neighbors were questioned. Nobody dressed as an Indian had been seen leaving Becker's house.

Fire investigators checked the arrow in the office. It was charcoal. In the bushes they discovered another arrow that missed the principal's office. It housed a long melted tube that held gasoline. No fingerprints. A few days later, the arson lab showed that surgical gloves were used. The arsonist was free. Eventually the heat was off Rodney Becker for arson. He would have to face assault charges for the gym incident.

Contractors arrived to assess the damage on Middleborough High. Estimates swelled to over 200,000 dollars, a first-class felony. The principal, vice principal and guidance counselors were housed in temporary trailers adjacent to the front offices. They walked up rusty, shaking steps to the 'Temp Building", every morning at seven. A new wing was to be built the following year. Rod didn't get into any fights or known trouble for months.

It was June and finals began. Students were ushered out of McDonald's at closing. Eyes were shutting throughout the days preceding tests. Coffee cups and exhausted students were everywhere.

Rod created an elaborate rolling statue he named "The Good Luck Duck." The Duck was an immaculate, metal-framed fiberglass sculpture that the driven young man conceived in his garage. He worked till early morning hours for a month. This brilliant work of art was the size of a grown man. Its sleek egg white ceramic surface with an orange bill made it museum material. Details like circular nostrils were on the bill. It's rough, webbed, orange toes had sleek claws extending out. The duck had one carved out pocket. Rod stocked it with hundreds of pens, pencils, White-Out and notepads saying, "Good Luck."

He would tow his creation to school every day during finals with a thick metal chain wrapped around his chest, padding it with two grey bath towels. Rod would endure marching several blocks, sweat-filled by the time he reached the gym doors. An oversized wooden cart showed up outside of the high school every day during final's week. The newspapers lauded it. Rod was famous again but not for biting an ear in wrestling or scoring three rushing touchdowns in the State Championship.

Two students with metal chains around their necks and tattoos stomped out their cigarettes near the duck. Rod was busy putting down his carrying chain. He stuffed his towel in a compartment on the back of the duck.

"How long did this thing take to build?" a lanky, freckled faced student with a yellow bow in her hair said to Rod.

"Oh! hi Lori." He took time to catch his breath. Smiling brightly, Rod began,

"It took about a month. Mom was calling me after one in the morning and I usually started at six."

"Wow. That's real perseverance."

Rod continued, "He bids you good luck" on your finals.

"Oh thanks. Bye", she said, not wanting to keep the conversation alive.

While discussing school policy in the library, the vice principal whispered to principal Durbin while pointing to Rod and the "Good Luck Duck." "The idiot is doing something productive. You're counting the days right?"

"Yeah. Until he finds something else to trouble us with," the principal said.

Finals week arrived. The Physics teacher practically hugged Rod's desk throughout the tests. He made the student-athlete roll up his sleeves twice. Rod checked box after box on the answer sheet without looking across his desk at the questions. The irritated teacher looked for cheat sheets up his sleeve, under his arm and on his jeans. He concealed a

42

video camera inside some Staples paper boxes on the far wall. Nothing. Rod appeared innocent, but the teacher remained in anguish.

Julio, Rod's sole friend despite their friendship-hatred-relationship was absent from school for a week. His father drives trucks interstate while his mother labors long hours managing a Taco Bell. In the summer following graduation, Vincent Terazano's friends trailed Rod and Julio to Seven-Eleven. They hid against the sidewalls. Two carried duffle bags. Vincent didn't forget the game where Rod permanently scarred his face by digging his nails under his facemask and biting him. Rod strolled out of Seven Eleven with a cup of green tea, two buttered rolls and a bag of chips. Eight powerful young men converged on him like an octopus' tentacles with chains, bats and clenched fists.

Rod bolted right. He threw his steaming tea at a crooked-nose teen, and then head butted him. The tough young man swung a bat to Rod's ribs. He groaned momentarily. Others swung at him with closed fists. After dodging them like he would players in a football game, he maneuvered his way up the adjoining fence to an Auto Body Repair shop. One foe grabbed his right foot. Rod kicked him downward in the face. He lunged safely over the tall fence. After rocketing through three backyards, Rod hid against a urine smelling garage until it was safe for him to go home. Julio was dragged from the car to the side of Seven-Eleven and beat unconscious.

The following afternoon Rod tried resting his back and fell into a deep sleep.

"It's Julio on the phone Rod", Lulu Becker called.

"What. Who's on?" Rod struggled.

Lulu's voice sounded like it was perpetually captured in a tunnel, "Julio...it's Julio...it's Julio, Rod."

Rod reached and finally found the phone.

Julio began, "You still owe me money."

"Sorry. I'll pay."

"I was cooking in the Good Luck Duck. You were going into dream college. It was your fault, 'friend.'" The word "friend" echoed out of Julio's mouth like a dying animal making one final appeal for help.

"Sorry."

Julio continued, "Did you hear, the principal is having emergency surgery."

"Durbin?"

"We only have one principal. Durbin had a head-on accident. A bottled gas truck turned the corner and slammed him."

Rod lay in bed, his eyes closed again. The phone rang one more time.

Lulu spoke again, "Rod. It's Mark on the phone."

"Mark who?"

"Mark Weinstein said you borrowed his book."

Rod began weeping quietly, "I need my sleep. What does everyone want with me?"

Lulu's voice faded out in the background.

He gripped the phone, looked at it, and then began with uncertainty, "Hello?"

"Hi Rodney." A troubled Mark Weinstein began. "It wasn't nice what you did to me."

"What did I do?"

"You stole the book I was taking out of the library."

"Stole the book?"

"Yes, stole the book, ripped it off, swiped it"

Rod couldn't reply.

"Now I'm getting notices from the library."

"Sorry. I'm having trouble. Can I pay you back if you can't find it?"

"Don't be so innocent. Everybody knows you."


Rod was pinned to the turf. The testimonies of those offended stared him in the eyes. The book was in his drawer a foot away.

"Mark I'll try…"

Mark slammed down the phone.

Rod put the phone back and reached in his drawer for the study guide.

It began ringing again. Rod was sure it was Mark.

Lulu called to Rod again, "Rod it's the principal's wife. Be nice."

"Hello."

A frail older woman began speaking, "This is Eileen Durbin."

Rod rubbed his lip, "Mrs. Durbin, someone told me about your husband. So sorry."

"Edwin's in the Emergency room with broken ribs. He has some internal bleeding."

"Sorry."

"He insisted on calling you."

There was silence.

"Please come to visit him. "He has some scholarship fund for you." She paused, shaking her head in disbelief, "Rodney, Edwin doesn't want you as his enemy."

"Oh, oh, I'll come with mom, I didn't mean anything. I'm stupid and suffer for it. He's a good man."

"Can you come to the hospital?"

Still in bed Rod put the phone down and reached down. He began lacing his shoes. Soon he plunged into a deep sleep.

The phone kept ringing while Rod slept.

Lulu's voice announced the call again, this time softly, "Rod, telephone."

Rod picked up the phone and began, "Hello."

A whispering defeated voice began, "He lost consciousness."

It was Principal Durbin's wife again, "You don't have to come."

Rod dropped the phone like it was on fire. He jumped away from it, and then pressed his hands against his head, squeezing it tightly.

Rod's mother jarred the door open. Two remote-controlled cars were pinned against it. The wheel snapped off one when she burst in. "Rod what's wrong?"

"It was Durbin's wife two times."

"What's wrong?"

"The principal's dying. He wanted to talk to me."

Lulu answered slowly, "How do you know?"

"That's why she called."

Lulu gazed at the fish tanks. Her eyes bounced off the wall clock then focused back to Rod.

"I thought you got rid of the cell?"

"I did. You told me to answer the phone."

"When?" Lulu answered, locking her arms.

"Just now."

Rod explored the room, then considered the calls and remembered Mark calling him.

"How about Mark's call?' Rod rubbed his hand against his lips. "Did Mark Weinstein call?"

"A few months ago he called, when you needed him." She looked around the room trying to give hope to Rod and to herself. "Something about football statistics."

"He didn't call today either."

She put her arm on his shoulder rubbing slowly.

Rod tore the dart filled picture of Principal Durbin and himself off the wall. He wept silently like he did when his grandfather died.

The most powerful, once undefeated young man in the county, ordinarily bronze skinned, turned pale. "I was sure Mark called about an overdue book then the principal's wife called about some accident he got in. I think she called twice."

"Lu…! Can you call Hopkins Medical Center?"

"She never called."

"She must have. I really feel the principal got into an accident. It was so real."

"I have the number."

Lulu popped a chocolate in her mouth and her phone book out from the console in the kitchen.

Rod called Plainview Medical Center and three neighboring hospitals. Principal Durbin never stepped in any.

Rodney was glued to his bed. Slow tears crawled down his anemic face.

Lulu brought in a wine glass filled to the top with ice water, "Rod, take this. You need rest. This isn't you."

For the first time in his life, the powerful youth began regularly chewing his nails, a habit that would endure. In a week his fingertips were chewed raw. Rod paced the yard during the long daytime hours. He shuffled inside the house when he saw a squirrel, birds or a bee approaching. Night grew worse. Students he had fought in the bowling alley met him. Football players and misdeeds from childhood took turns poking at him. Rod's appetite was normally greater than a starving tiger. Now he could barely swallow a few pieces of toast and sip soup. He lost interest in everything, refusing friends and his mom's visitors. Nightmares continued. The tormented teen was afraid to sleep. Rod's mother contacted a sleep clinic. Rod hated doctors. Haunting scenes and people refused to stop coming. Principal Durbin, girls he dated, a man in the park, an elderly cripple, two students from neighboring high schools lined up in his bedroom taking turns to be on his sleep screen. A lame cat he threw rocks at when he was nine howled out in distress.

One hundred and eight pound Lulu Becker tackled Rod when he lay on the grass in the backyard and hauled him in. "You're embarrassing both of us", she whispered.

Rod ducked behind trees. Lulu screened phone calls. She reassured friends, "He's not feeling well lately." Neighbors noticed the athlete shrink. In a month Rod was scheduled to begin classes at the University. Rod was forced into the jeans he left in ninth grade.

Except for mail, only Lulu answered the door during the daytime.

One bright morning at ten, an urgent tapping came on Becker's home. Lulu was shopping. It was Mr. Fae, the white haired, blind man and his German Shepherd, Gloria. He was wearing corduroy pants, a checkered shirt with dark sunglasses and a Coke baseball cap.

"What could he want?" Rod considered, spying through the bay window.

Then he ran out of options and pried the door open a crack.

"Hi, Mr. Fae."

"Hi, Rod. Can we chat?"

Rod got a cold chill. "I'm not feeling good lately." He began shutting the door.

Mr. Fae pushed his aluminum walking cane in the door as if he could see or sense the door was shutting.

Through the small opening Mr. Fae continued, "That's why I'm here. I'd like to help you."

Rod considered, "Why would he help me?" Mr. Fae always boasted about Rod being a star athlete when he walked past his house with his daughter. Now Rod felt guilty about the blind jokes he told his friends. Whenever they saw Mr. Fae's daughter, Sandy, in school he had a handful of blind jokes. She overheard many of them. Rod thought, "He's getting into my space. All the jokes I told about him. Why would he bother with a creep like me?"

He took a chance, "Please come in. Sit down here Mr. Fae."

With the spark of a toddler in a department store, Rod felt hope. "Does Gloria want something to eat?"

"No, I feed her after we walk in the morning." Mr. Fae petted his dog, as she sniffed, scanning inside of the Becker's home.

"This way."

The troubled youth ushered the blind man and his dog into the carpeted living room.

Mr. Fae swung his cane around. Gloria panted a foot away, probing the living room from top to bottom.

A fluffy white sofa set was surrounded by two mammoth vases with ten-foot miniature walnut trees bursting out. The ceiling was a high panoramic window opened to the street.

"Sit here." Rod began.

Mr. Fae continued, "I want to talk to you about your problem."

"You know I have a problem?"

"Yes, I do."

He walked Mr. Fae over and patted the sofa. Mr. Fae's walking cane hit a glass-topped coffee table, then the sofa. He ran his fingers the length of the sofa then repositioned himself and sat. Rod sat on a loveseat diagonally facing the sofa. Gloria gingerly sat between the coffee table and Mr. Fae. Gloria swung her head in semicircles two times. She then peered at Rod and laid on her paws.

Rod looked at a hope filled man's face, then glimpsed down at Gloria. He opened up, "I've trouble sleeping lately."

Mr. Fae said, "Neighbors noticed you lost weight." His head turned towards Rod.

Tears raced down Rod's face, "I don't know what to do," he pleaded.

Reaching across the table Mr. Fae covered Rod's hand. Gloria poked her head up. She growled slightly uncomfortable with both hands touching.

To assure her all was fine, Mr. Fae patted her head.

He then began, "Sounds to me like you want to get on with your life."

Rod shook his head, "I'm the problem."

"But Rodney, you can talk to the principal."

Rod looked around the room and considered, 'How could he know about the dreams?' Then he spoke out, "He must hate my guts."

Rod stood up, breaking loose from Mr. Fae's hands. Gloria got up on all fours with a mild growl, observing Rod like a bear protecting its cub. Rod combed his hair with his fingers. "He would probably love it, if he hears the condition I'm in."

Mr. Fae shook his head, "No. I know the principal well. Let's go to his home."

"What? Just keep walking in front of his house, waiting for him to come home?"

"No." Mr. Fae said, smiling and shaking his head. "Rod, he gets home at quarter to four each day."

Rod attempted to reply but stuttered, while chewing his nails.

"He still shows up at school each day."

The next day at three twenty Mr. Fae and Gloria faithfully stood at Becker's door. Gloria wagged her tail in the cool afternoon breeze.

Lulu Becker smiled brightly with puckered lips, new jeans and a polo shirt and opened the door.

"Hi, Mr. Fae. Rod said you'd be here. Thanks for coming."

"Hi Lulu. How's everything?" Mr. Fae said, calculatingly. His dark sunglasses reflected Rod's house back to Lulu.

She glimpsed back towards Rod's room and whispered, "Well you know. He's usually so independent, but now he needs someone. Wait a minute I'll get him."

Lulu shuffled over quickly to Rod's room.

"Rod."

"I'm nervous," Rod admitted.

"Rod something's gotta work." Lulu said, looking into Rod's acne covered face.

In a few minutes Mr. Fae, Gloria and Rod were pacing to Principal Durbin's ranch house about fifteen minutes away.

"If we go past we'll just circle around to see him."

Mr. Durbin's silver Oldsmobile pulled up just after four.

Mr. Fae looked towards the sky, "Is that you, Edwin?" Though he couldn't see he knew the sound of his car already.

The principal jolted out of his car, wearing a navy blue suit and a striped tie. Rod had trouble looking in his direction.

"Good afternoon gentlemen."

Mr. Durbin never called Rod a gentleman.

Rod glimpsed over to the car, "Hi Mr. Durbin. How's the school?"

The principal answered, "Better. Looks like you lost some weight."

Rod looked down, "Yea."

"Getting ready for college Rod?

"Yea. I may take a break."

Mr. Fae and Rod slowly walked towards principal Durbin's car. Mr. Durbin put his hand around Mr. Fae. His other hand reached out toward his house, "Come on in. Our retriever had puppies."

"Bring Gloria?" Mr. Fae asked, tugging on her silver chain. Gloria sat next to him on the driveway, panting.

"The retriever and her puppies are in the backyard. Gloria's safe in the house."

Mr. Durbin's wife stood in the doorway, squinting out at Mr. Fae and Rod in the driveway. She said, "What a surprise. Didn't think you'd come over Rodney. Hi Mr. Fae."

"Hello." Mr. Fae answered, cocking his head towards her.

Rod couldn't speak.

The men got together in the living room. Mrs. Durbin poured tea and homemade cookies. Within minutes Rod opened up, "Principal Durbin, I wasn't a good student. Sorry I caused you so much trouble."

The principal and Mrs. Durbin took a long look at each other. This was a transformed Rodney Becker.

"A caterpillar turned butterfly," Mrs. Durbin thought. Mr. Fae, an excellent public speaker and social worker orchestrated bringing two people together.

The principal gave Rodney a big hug, "Rodney I didn't think this nightmare would ever cease."

Rodney turned his head from side to side, "It's all over."

Mr. Fae added, "As the song goes, 'we've only just begun.'"

Upon arriving home, Lulu greeted Rod at the door, "How did it go?"

"We had some snacks and things are better. Hope Mr. Fae's advice works."

Lulu peeked in to see if everything was all right. Rod lay there with his sweats on, holding a milkshake.

He agreed to help with the principal's garden, and to install a greenhouse. That night the atmosphere changed in Rod's home. He wore a hot facemask and attempted sleeping under a heating blanket. Dentist music played instead of the noise he loved for years. On Rod's request, Lulu continued to sit on a stool outside of his room. She gobbled Godiva chocolates, read some fashion magazines, awaiting the usual scream from the nightmares and the backrub that ensued. No screams came at one, two, two-thirty. She fell asleep against the wall at two-forty five. Lulu crawled into bed at three.

That night attempting to undo his torment, Rod sat in his swivel chair, calling Mark Weinstein.

"Hello is this Mark?"

"Speaking."

"This is Rod Becker."

"Hi Rod." Mark paused for several seconds. All that could be heard was a health program on Mark's TV. Mark finally continued, "What's the reason for the call?"

"Mark, thanks for helping me in Algebra in High School. Without you I wouldn't have passed."

"You're welcome. If I could help again, let me know."

"I really called to apologize for stealing the study guide."

They both hung on speechless then Mark answered, "I figured you did."

"What do I owe you?"

"I think it came to seven dollars."

"I'll pay. Please forgive me."

"People have done worse to me. I forgive."

He woke up a different person, "Mom, what's for breakfast?"

She began mixing batter and made some pancakes with strawberries, a vanilla milkshake and orange juice.

Rod called and made reparations to twenty-three people in the next week.

An elderly lady screamed and cried at Rod for over a half an hour, refusing reconciliation. Two ex-girlfriends hung up on him. A local store owner Rod troubled invited him to a small café to eat breakfast. Several accepted his sincere apologies. Some didn't trust his motives, while the others were shocked when he called. He refused to date any girl for fear of hurting one. During sports he was polite and considered others before himself.

Rodney Becker became a household member of the Durbin family. They bowled, went fishing and occasionally ate dinner together. Emotionally the young athlete was able to put it all together in a University setting. Rod drove off to Colorado as a disciplined freshman. His knee was injured during football and a few months later had surgery. During his rehabilitation time Rod volunteered to work with the blind. He called Edwin Durbin and Mr. Fae on weekends. Edwin Durbin, his wife, Mr. Fae's family and Rod's parents attended graduation at Western State College in Colorado. With incredible upper body strength and a transformed spirit Rod made it to the Olympic team as a wrestler. Rodney Becker was a bully no more.

# THANK YOU

Thank you dear reader for reading our book. You can check our other amazing picture books which include Unlikely Friends, The Mystery Box, and The Contest by James E. Benedict.

## Contact Information

Website: www.emmanuelliteracy.com

Writer: James Benedict : Emmanuelliteracyfoundation@gmail.com

Illustrator: Abhinav Gupta : abhinavarte@gmail.com

Lightning Source UK Ltd.
Milton Keynes UK
UKHW020729280721
387854UK00001B/2